HEART OF THE AJS

SIX WORLDS SAGA: STORY ONE

ENDORSEMENTS

Heart of the Ajs is a fantasy tale of the slickness of evil and the subtle strength of good. T. E. Bradford shows style in her writing and elegance in her description. An enjoyable read.
—**Ralene Burke**, fantasy author, *Sacred Armor Trilogy*

I thoroughly enjoyed *Heart of the Ajs* from start to finish. Fantastic character development, masterful world building, and a beautiful story that leaves me wanting to read more about this new literary universe. T. E. Bradford is a master. I can't wait to see what she comes out with next.
—**James Quinlan Meservy**, author, the *Rai Saga*

T. E. Bradford shows masterly skill and weaving the world in *Heart of the Ajs*. She creates a world that is both foreign and familiar, inviting me to care for her characters. A refreshingly different sort of read.
—**Bokerah Brumley**, author, *Keepers of New Haven* series.

Heart of the Ajs is a solid read and set in a world much fuller and more vibrant than can be expressed in so short a story. I look forward to other opportunities to explore the world of Bradford's creation.
—**Jeremy Bullard**, author, *Realms of Our Own* and *Facets of Reality* series.

HEART OF THE AJS

SIX WORLDS SAGA: STORY ONE

T. E. BRADFORD

ELK LAKE PUBLISHING INC
Plymouth, Massachusetts

Cover and Interior Design: T.E. Bradford, Derinda Babcock

Editor(s): Linda Rondeau, Deb Haggerty

Author Represented By:

PUBLISHED BY: Elk Lake Publishing, Inc., 35 Dogwood Drive, Plymouth, MA 02360, 2019

Library Cataloging Data

Names: Bradford, T. E. (T. E. Bradford)

Heart of the Ajs—Six Worlds Saga: Story One / T. E. Bradford

52 p. 23cm × 15cm (9in × 6 in.)

Description: She's to be married to the evil Ajs. Can she save her world?

Identifiers: ISBN-13: 978-1-951080-21-1 (trade) | 978-1-951080-22-8 (POD)

| 978-1-951080-23-5 (e-book)

Key Words: Speculative, other worlds, honor, evil, good, spiritual warfare, family

LCCN: 2019945609 Fiction

DEDICATION

Alicia and Marje—you are as precious as Asfari pearls.

ACKNOWLEDGMENTS

God doesn't always say yes. Sometimes he says no, or maybe … or wait. When we don't get the things we hope for, it's easy to feel disappointed, but God promises He has plans to prosper us and not to harm us. He always answers the prayers of His children, and He knows not only what we want, but what we need.

Thank you, Heavenly Father, for giving me the opportunity to share the wonder of your awesome universe with others. Thank you for the husband you crafted especially for me, and the son that is the best parts of both of us.

An enormous thank you to Deb Haggerty and Elk Lake Publishing, Inc. for believing not only in my stories, but in me. I am so very blessed to be part of such a talented, faithful group of people that are truly a second family.

Linda Rondeau, my patient and fervent editor, thank you for not only helping make my work shine, but teaching me to be a better writer. Pointing out people's mistakes can be tricky, delicate work. You make walking the tightrope look easy.

Soleil, Carole, Lindsey-Jane, Larry, James, Ally … I have many wonderful writing friends all over the world thanks to the internet, but none better than all of you. Everyone at Deep Magic, Dan, Kristin, Jeff, and to the people who encourage and lift me up in prayer—Shelli, Beckie Lindsey, thank you for being part of my journey.

Alicia and Marje, I don't know if you know how important you are, not only to my process but to me. Your spirit truly shines. Your friendship uplifts me, and your constant eagerness to read my work encourages me to keep going. Everyone should have friends like you in their lives. I'm sure glad I do.

HIDDEN POWER - ALQUAT ALKHAFIA

الطاقة المخفية

"He has no heart!"

Saba's face paled. "Do not speak such words, Nafisa." She made the sign of warding, kissing her fingertips and drawing the symbol of the sacred eye of Roshu in the air.

"He is the Ajs—a chosen leader, Saba. Not a mystic. He cannot see or hear us."

Saba's eyes widened, so much white showing Nafisa feared they might escape their sockets.

"He is yunfah." Saba's voice was barely loud enough to hear, and trembled in rhythm to her shaking body.

Nafisa snorted. "Stories told to children. There is no such thing as one who can control the air itself. Yunfah is only a legend."

Saba's face darkened, her brows pulling down over eyes still round with fear. "You are zaman. You should know better than anyone such power is no mere legend."

Nafisa threw her hands up in frustration. "It is because I am called zaman that I know it is nothing more."

All her life she had heard the same thing. "You are zaman, Nafisa … You hold incredible power, Nafisa."

Pah!

If she had any power she was wont to see it.

"You tempt fate."

Fate. There was another word Nafisa doubted. "Does fate stuff my father's pockets with gold?" She scoffed. "The Ajs An'hlj harvests the Asfari people like grain. Is it fate which convinces my father to ignore their cries or the jewels An'hlj sprinkles like salt on his fingers and his head?"

"Fate does not care whether or not you believe, Nafisa. It will still come when invited by your words and your heart."

"Then let it come." Anger flamed inside her like a wildfire. "Let the Ajs come with it. I will rebuke them both."

Saba shook her head in disbelief. "I love you like a daughter, Nafisa, but I cannot protect you from yourself."

"Nor will you need to." Nafisa walked away before she could hurt Saba with her words.

Nafisa's handmaid since birth, Saba was indeed like a mother to her. Yet while incredibly caring, the woman was also disturbingly fearful. Her superstition ate at Nafisa like a bad tooth she could not stop probing.

She closed the door behind her as she left the room, unaware of her destination until she turned down the hallway to her father's musalla. He spent more and more time in his worship room, consulting his precious sakhra. This object too had come from the Ajs. A piece of the morning star. Whatever the sakhra truly was, trouble had come along with it.

Nafisa pushed aside the shimmering curtains and barged into the room, but the cushions scattered around the floor were all empty. She dropped to her knees beside the stone altar of Eloah, its sun-shaped face glowing in the afternoon light.

"Eloah, Eternal God, give me wisdom."

She walked to the opposite doorway, leaning her head out into the hall. "Father?" Her voice echoed back to her.

She sighed through clenched teeth. He could not hide from her. She would not go quietly while he sold her future to a shaytan.

A soft hissing sound reached her ears.

Snakes could get in under doors or through small holes. She turned, scanning the floor—nothing.

The hissing came again.

Nafisa stilled.

The sound came from the alcove where her father kept the sakhra, hidden behind a piece of plain linen. Nafisa stared at the white square, the moisture in her mouth draining away as the hissing sound came again. Her heart pounded against her ribs.

Could a snake have gotten into the alcove? The space was small, but perhaps the snake was small.

In her heart, she didn't believe the sound came from any creature. Hand shaking, Nafisa reached out to pull back the linen. No snake hid in the small space. Only the black sakhra sat at the center of the alcove on a carved pedestal, ebon surface glossy and smooth as glass, drinking in the light and returning only darkness. As she stared, the hissing resumed. The stone swelled and slowly deflated.

"Sharun!" Nafisa reeled back, making the sign of the sacred eye in the air.

This was no piece of star. This was an evil thing, dark and malevolent.

Touch it.

Nafisa gasped and dropped the linen. The cloth fell back into place, shielding the sakhra from view, but the air was heavy. She heard a rustle and knew the stone moved. Icy fear gripped her.

"I am no better than Saba," she whispered, taking a shuddering breath.

Her father had procured countless teachers to show her how to use her gift. They had given her at least one useful skill. Nafisa used the calming technique now, breathing in deeply through her nose and exhaling through her mouth. She focused on one part of her body at a time, releasing tension with each exhalation. Her heart still thumped against her rib cage, but the beat mirrored in her throat slowed to a more normal tempo.

Carefully, she reached out and pulled the linen back again. "It's just a rock."

The stone swelled and deflated, defying her declaration.

Claim it. One touch and its power will be yours.

The unfamiliar voice spoke in her head.

One touch.

A man's voice, deep and rough, yet compelling. She wanted to touch the black rock, to trace her fingers along the smooth surface. Her hand inched closer, already knowing how the glass-like planes would feel against her skin. How cool to the touch, soothing and powerful, and—

Nafisa jerked her hand away.

What dark magic was this? How could a voice in her head make her want to do something against her own will?

"Nafisa!"

She spun to find her father standing behind her, face taut. Graying brows pushed low over dark eyes. His lips pinched together, the corners curved down toward a chin covered in whiskers more white than black.

When had her father grown old?

"What are you doing?"

She took a breath to steady herself. "I was looking for you."

His eyes narrowed. "I am not in the alcove."

She stifled a nervous laugh. "I heard something. I thought it might be a snake."

His eyes flickered at her words, and her heart skipped a beat. Did he know? Had he heard the sound before?

His face softened. "You should have called a servant. You could have been bitten."

"I'm sorry, Father."

He nodded, placated by her explanation, and lowered himself onto one of the large cushions. "Why were you looking for me?"

"You know why."

His eyes flicked back to hers, a trace of uncertainty in their dark surface. "Saba told you, did she?"

"Of course. As you commanded her."

"Then you know my word is law. Your fate no longer rests with me."

Her hands balled into fists. "You sold me to the Ajs."

"I did no such thing. I made an arrangement of marriage, as you know."

Anger flamed into fury. "You did not even ask me."

"I am your father." Though he shouted, his words lacked any real conviction. "Fathers do not ask their children for permission. Your life belongs to me."

"Not anymore."

"No," he said with a sigh.

Nafisa's lips trembled. "You care for me so little?" Tears stung her eyes. "Have you no love left in your heart for your daughter?"

He lifted his hands. "My love for you is why I have done this, Nafisa. The Ajs is the most powerful man in the quadrant. He holds the keys to the sky gate. As his wife, all he possesses will also be yours."

Was her father truly so naïve?

"He works his fields with slaves. He trades their children to other worlds! Do you truly think he will be generous with his wife?"

Father's eyes flickered again with what she hoped was a trace of doubt. What had the Ajs promised for Nafisa's hand? Certainly more than trinkets. Had he promised grandchildren who would be future rulers?

Nafisa fell to her knees. "You are wise, my father. You have always told me to think carefully, for the hearts of others are never entirely what they seem. Yet, now you tell me this man, this shaytan, will keep his promises?" She shook her head. "He will not. He will use us and leave us to rot in the dirt."

She buried her face against her father's knees as hot tears came.

"Nafisa." He stroked her hair. "Do not be troubled."

She lifted her tear-streaked face. "How can I not be?"

He cupped her chin in his hand. "I have prayed for Eloah to guide us, my daughter. He has revealed to me the heart of the Ajs."

She did not understand.

"An'hlj is thirsty for power, of this you speak truly. But you need not fear." He brushed the back of his hand along her cheek. "You are zaman, the holder of time, defender of the sun. You hold the power of Eloah himself. Enough power to bring even the Ajs to his knees if you could but discover the key to release what is inside you."

The warmth of his caress turned cold.

Power? Was this the heart of their arrangement?

The pieces fell into place like a pezzel. The Ajs wanted her power for himself. He thought her a weapon. The surprise would be on him. This dagger had no blade. She was an empty sheath, useless and wasted.

"He longs to share his passion with someone," her father murmured. "You can be that person, Nafisa. Be his wife. Be his soul."

"How do you know what he longs for?" She shook her head in despair, looking back when her father did not answer.

His eyes danced away from hers. He fiddled with a piece of her hair. "I just do."

Her worry and anger hardened into fear. "How, Father?"

Again he did not answer. Instead, his eyes flicked to a point over her shoulder. She did not have to turn to know where his gaze landed. Faintly, from behind, she heard the rasp as the sakhra moved. In and out. Pulsing. Beating …

Breathing.

She sprang to her feet, her balance swaying from the sudden movement. She placed her hand on the wall to steady herself. Surely her senses betrayed her.

"Nafisa?" Her father reached for her, face filled with concern, yet his eyes betrayed him.

"What have you done?"

He swallowed, turning from her gaze, but Nafisa had already seen the truth.

"Did the sakhra whisper to you?"

The blood drained from his face, leaving him as pale as the linen covering the alcove.

"What did it say?"

"Stop." Her father's voice was strangled.

"Did you touch it?"

His eyes widened, giving her his answer. He licked his lips. "It is not what you think, Nafisa."

She grabbed his arm. "Tell me, Father. Has he poisoned you? Used the sakhra to keep you in his thrall?"

"No." Her father wrenched his arm away.

"Then what?"

The hissing came again and he stilled, tipping his head to the side as if listening. "You already know." He said, his tone flat.

Dread washed down her limbs and surged through her middle, leaving a frozen wasteland behind.

She did know.

The black rock was precisely as the Ajs had told them—a piece of a star. Hadn't she heard how An'hlj had fallen from the sky, a gift to his people? How he'd arrived with the device which had opened up their trade and their future in the form of the sky gate? He was a star, fallen from the heavens. The hard, cold black rock sitting in the alcove was a piece of that star.

The Ajs An'hlj was sharun, the black stone was his dark heart.

SERPENT—AFEAA

أفعى

"He's here."

As if summoned by the words, horns sounded, their echo coming from the direction of the Shultan's receiving hall and throne room.

Saba's eyes widened as she turned to face her mistress. "You knew?"

Nafisa picked up a fig, wanting to rinse the taste from her mouth, but even the sweet fruit could not cleanse the bitter film coating her tongue. Even the air, already hot though the sun was barely above the horizon, felt heavy with portent. The birds did not sing. The insects did not buzz. All the world held its breath.

"Come." Spots of red stood out on Saba's ashen face. "You must prepare." She poured the last jug of steaming water into the tub and motioned for Nafisa to get in.

The steam was fragrant with cimmeron and ginjir. Nafisa lowered herself into the water. The warmed scents pricked at her nose, spicy yet soothing in their familiarity.

"You would turn me into a dish to be served up."

Saba did not answer. Instead, she lifted Nafisa's arm, rubbing yasimin oil into the skin above her elbow. The deep, rich fragrance of vanilla filled the air as Saba's deft fingers massaged each muscle and tender pressure point down to the wrist. Normally Nafisa would have sighed with pleasure, head laid back to savor such relaxing treatment. Not today. Today nothing could soothe her tension.

A terrible vision had troubled her sleep. In her dream, shadows chased her through caverns lit by fire, writhing shapes curling along walls and stone floors, their sound a sibilant hiss. She ran, bare feet pierced by sharp rocks, leaving bloody prints to mark her passing. The hissing grew louder, the shadows drawn by her blood. She ran, stumbling as the floor shifted, forcing her along the cavern wall as the shadows flowed closer. Terror filled her throat, the metallic taste of fear thick in her mouth.

The floor opened up beneath her and she was falling … only instead of falling down into a cavity, she fell upward. Her body slammed against the roof of the tunnel, shale raining down around her. Fragments caught in her hair, thick dust forcing her to close her eyes. She fought to open them again, grit coating her eyelashes … but she had to look. Had to see. The shadows writhed closer, slithering up the rock walls, surrounding her with one massive, squirming ring. She watched in horror as one looped around her ankle, its ethereal form sinuous and wet. Yet, instead of expected cold, the shadows burned her flesh like acid. She opened her mouth to scream. A shadow slithered across her face, darting between her lips, filling her airway, and burning its way into her chest. Fiery fingers filled her lungs, spreading outward, searching every nook and crevice, scorching away every trace of life.

She'd awoken gasping for air, clutching the silk fabric of her shift as she sucked in deep breaths.

The moment her eyes opened, she'd known the Ajs had arrived. His presence on her home world was a violation—as much a trespass as the shadow that had filled her throat. He would choke the life from her people as the nightmare shadows had choked the air from her lungs. Her terrible dream was but a foretaste of what was to come. Reality would be far worse. She could still feel the blaze in her throat and the horrible sensation of a presence not her own deep within.

Rather than soothing, the warm bath sucked all trace of energy from her limbs. She sat, unable to resist as Saba painted her body with henna. Carefully, the handmaid marked Nafisa's skin with promises of truth, obedience, and fidelity.

To my people, she promised, the only rebellion she could manage. Not to him.

Her eyes were lined with kohl. She was draped in silks and dusted with jewels until her body sparkled. Saba plaited her hair into a thick braid and seeded the strands with Asfari pearls ranging in size from grains of rice to olive pits. Gold and copper leaf coated her eyelids and brows all the way to her hairline. A headdress of golden chains was carefully draped from her crown to below her chin. Lastly, the henna tattoos on her hands were traced with liquid gold, shining lines of decoration glittering around each finger like a painted-on glove.

Saba stood back, taking in her handiwork. "You are ready."

As ready as she could be. How did one prepare to face the darkness?

With bells, apparently. Nafisa jingled as she stood from the chair, her muscles protesting having stayed so long in one position. She was tempted to remove the anklets, but the weight, like shackles, seemed somehow appropriate.

A knock came at the door. Saba hurried to open it.

One of her father's men stood outside. His eyes flicked nervously to Nafisa, and he bowed as if to hide his face. "The Shultan requires you."

Of course he did.

Nafisa said nothing. She merely followed as her father's guard turned and started walking. Saba grabbed Nafisa's hand.

"Nafisa." Her voice trembled. "Remember who you are."

Nafisa wanted to be angry, but her heart softened when she saw the fear pooled in Saba's dark eyes.

Nafisa nodded. "I know who I am."

Saba released Nafisa's hand, motioning for her to follow the guard who hurried ahead, rushing her headlong into a nightmare.

They stopped at the side entrance to the great hall. Inside, her father would be seated on his jeweled throne, honored guest at his right hand. The guard knocked. An answering knock came from the other side, and the doors swung inward.

A greasy feeling rested in the pit of her stomach, threatening to send its meager contents back out. She balled her fists, swallowing back her anger and disgust. She would not be cowed. She was Nafisa El Farouz, the daughter of the greatest Shultan in all of Asfar. Perhaps in all the six worlds of Baqa. If the Ajs An'hlj thought she would give herself without a fight, he was mistaken. Lifting her head high, Nafisa entered her father's hall.

The carpet drank the sound of her steps. She refused to look at the dais until she reached the center of the room. Breathing full and even, she forced herself to remain calm against the riot of emotions threatening to overwhelm her. Even a hint of fear would be too much. Her people depended on her to be strong.

She stopped. The light from the high windows shone down. She was the defender of the sun. She was zaman.

Firmly, and without hesitation, Nafisa turned.

He could have been handsome. Long dark hair lay full against skin the color of nutmeg, twin braids at his temples. His beard was likewise braided beneath full lips. Pulled-back locks revealed a face marked on either side with symbols—symbols she should recognize but did not. Only the one centered above his eyes was familiar.

The sacred eye of Roshu, he who had looked upon the face of Eloah the Eternal God, only in this depiction the image was pierced with a spear. Drops of ink imitated dripping blood, tracking down into thick brows capping eyes that should have been dark and mysterious. Instead they glowed a sickly yellow. At their center, irises the shape of four-armed stars expanded outward, the markings staining the white with dark blots.

"Nafisa." He said only her name, yet her skin crawled as if a thousand insects scuttled over her body.

Beside him, the Shultan sat on his jeweled throne, face slack and eyes unfocused.

Father.

What had this serpent done to him? Anger burned through her fear. Carefully, every step precise and steady, she walked closer. She stopped at the bottom step, a length from the creature coiled above her. She did not fool herself into thinking he could not strike even from there, but the distance gave her a small measure of comfort.

"You are the Ajs."

His lips twisted. "And you are my bride."

Loathing made her want to spit. "So I have been told."

His brows twitched. "Your father is a wise man."

She glanced at him. "My father is a good man." At least he was. "You have certainly … influenced him."

An'hlj gave a deep, sweeping bow. She had not realized how tall he was.

"It was not a compliment."

"I know."

"Whatever my father has told you, I do not agree with his choice in this." She kept her gaze steady. "I will not be a willing partner."

His smile was wide and vicious. "Then I chose well."

Everything about him screamed sickness and blasphemy.

Her father rose to his feet, drawing her eyes away from the profane visage.

"Daughter," he said, his voice thick and unnatural, "you will depart at the moon's rising. Gather what you will."

Steeling herself, she took the last few steps, leaning in to kiss her father's cheek, his skin, cool and stiff as death.

She recoiled in horror, turning back to the Ajs. "What have you done to him?"

His eyes widened. "I?"

"If you hurt him …"

Quick as a darting shadow, he stood beside her, lips against her ear. "Your obedience assures his life." His whisper was soft and hot. "As long as you fulfill your duty, he will be safe."

She took the moment to look into those glowing, desecrated eyes. "What do you want from me?"

His tongue flicked out like a snake's, brushing her cheek. "A mere taste, Princess."

Against her will, her body trembled. She pulled away, backing down the steps. The guards looked on, faces uncertain.

"Until the moon's rising, my beloved." The Ajs lowered his head, but his eyes never left hers.

Nafisa held herself rigid until she reached the doors. Only when they closed behind her did she loose her control, body quaking as she turned and ran.

DESTRUCTION - TADMIR

تدمير

"I will kill him."

Saba sat on Nafisa's bed, face drawn. Her hands flexed as she clenched them in her lap. "You must not say such things."

Nafisa gaped at her handmaid and threw her arms into the air. "Not say such things? My father, the Shultan is in his thrall. An'hlj threatens harm if I do not obey."

"Even more reason to stay your hand." Saba looked up, dark eyes troubled. "You have been promised. To refuse now is the breaking of a trust. Such actions could spell the Shultan's doom."

"Not acting will spell all our dooms." A storm raged within her, and Nafisa's anger crashed like thunder.

Saba jumped to her feet. "What about your people?"

The charge of lightning filled her nostrils. "You mean those he uses as slaves? Those whose families are torn apart so he can profit? Families like my own?"

"The Ajs holds the key to the sky gate. What will happen to your family when there is no more food? No more water?"

"We will find another way once he is gone. Without him we will be stronger."

"Asfar has become a desert. Without him, we will all die." Saba's body shook.

Nafisa had never seen Saba react so strongly. Could the woman be right? Would they all die without the Ajs's wretched sky gate? Was giving in to him the only way to save their people?

"No. There must be another way." There must be. Eloah save them.

Saba gripped Nafisa's arms. "You are zaman, but you are also the Shultan's daughter. You must consider your people above all else. Above your father. Above even yourself."

Shock and grief stabbed at her heart. Did Saba truly believe Nafisa would put her own wants above her people? Did the woman who had raised her like a mother know her heart so little? Her people were the reason she must act. She must destroy this sharun, for truly he was evil incarnate. While he lived, her people would only suffer.

Nafisa pulled her arms free from Saba's grip. Wordlessly she turned and walked away, unable to look for another moment at the face of someone who would believe her so selfish. So rash. Nafisa had thought of little else but her people. Her people were the very reason why she did not want to marry An'hlj. His treatment of them revealed his dark nature. She had always believed so.

Now, having seen him with her own eyes, she knew she was right. The Ajs was beyond corrupt. He was vile. An abomination. With him in control, her people might exist for a while, but they would see their children sold. Their men broken and beaten. Their women used and discarded. This was no life.

Nafisa stopped at the doorway to her father's musalla. Her feet had brought her back to this place. She pushed aside the curtains, half expecting An'hlj to be here waiting for her, his mouth twisted in a terrible smile of triumph. But, the room was empty. Her footsteps whispered as she crossed to the alcove.

The white linen square hung unmoving. No sound came from within. A sudden panic seized her. What if her father had moved the sakhra, hidden it somewhere? What if the Ajs had reclaimed his stone, dark purpose fulfilled? With shaking fingers, she swept back the cloth.

The black rock sat cool and silent. Unmoving. Unbreathing.

"You cannot fool me," Nafisa whispered. "I know what you are."

She waited for the voice to echo in her head, urging her to touch the glossy surface.

No voice came.

Why did the heart not speak? Was this some trick? Had the sakhra turned back to mere stone?

No. She would not be lulled. This devilry would not keep her from doing what she must. Destroy the heart, destroy the man. All she need do was smash the chunk against the floor. Smash it into dust and rubble. She would have to touch the rock, but she would go quickly. Destroy the stone before its sharun influence could work on her.

Doubt niggled. What if destroying the heart did not kill him? His rage would be insurmountable. His vindication warranted. He would punish her through her father and her people. They would pay the price if she made a mistake. She knew this without doubt. If destroying the sakhra did not kill the Ajs, their lives would be forfeit. Was she ready for this? Was she ready to die for a mere chance at freedom for her people?

Yes.

Nafisa held her hands as steady as she could and grasped the obsidian rock.

The sakhra surged to life. The smooth surface, cool in her grip, pulsed and glowed. A dark presence probed her mind. Vaporous fingers writhed in the air all around her, unseen, yet with substance, shifting, moving, covering every inch of her.

Unlike the dream, she could still breathe. The shadows did not burn … but she couldn't keep them from working their way inside her, from invading her nostrils, her ears, even her skin and hair. She sensed them scrabbling to find purchase but unable to access anything beyond the physical. Unable to gain dominance.

Nafisa's mind was her own. Her actions did not betray her. Whatever dark thrall controlled her father had not worked on her. She was not a puppet to the Ajs.

With a feral grin, she lifted the sakhra over her head. He could not stop her. She would smash the stone into dust and let the wind blow every fragment of him away. She was zaman, the holder of time—she could not be bound by his current of magic. She held his very heart in her hands. The heart of the Ajs.

The heart of the Ajs.

Nafisa stilled.

The heart's magic had not consumed her. Did not control her. She trembled on the edge of a revelation. She could feel the stone's magic —An'hlj's magic—inside her, yet separate. She held the foreign awareness apart from her own, containing both without allowing one to rule the other. Without allowing his magic to corrupt her.

What had the heart whispered to her before?

One touch and its power will be yours.

Could this be true? Could the power connecting the ebon rock to the Ajs work both ways? Perhaps she did not have to destroy it. Perhaps there was another way.

Slowly, she lowered her arms. In her hands, the black stone pulsed and shone … but Nafisa was no longer afraid.

INTO THE SKY – FI ALSAMA

في السماء

The moon rose like a ripe melon, swollen with promise. Nafisa gripped the arms of the seat as she looked out at the dark sky.

"Have you flown before?" The pilot, also likely her guard, turned to face her as she fastened some kind of harness.

The woman's milky skin and yellow hair were a shock to Nafisa. Yellow was the color of fruits and flowers, not hair. The spiky strands stood atop her head like a thousand rigid little spears, leaving Nafisa to guess how her strange companion defied gravity to keep them there.

"I have never travelled outside of Asfar."

The woman's pale brows lifted. She made a whistling noise with her teeth. "Oh. This will be a real adventure for you then."

She pressed a button and a dull roar filled the air.

"Engines." Her companion said with a smile. "They'll quiet down after we lift off."

Lift off? "Is An'hlj not coming with us?"

"Just us." The pilot swept her arm at the transparent panels around them. "The Ajs wanted to be sure you were able to appreciate the view. His larger ship is a cargo. Not many viewports."

Nafisa nodded as if the words made sense. More likely the Ajs wanted her to see the vastness of space and know she could not escape him. She was trapped into whatever demise he had in store for her.

A moment later the term lift off became clear as the craft rose above the ground. Although not altogether unpleasant, the sensation of being afloat without water disoriented her.

"Ready?" The woman pressed a button on the panel in front of her, placing her palms on two flat surfaces suspended above. She tilted them forward.

The ship leapt ahead and upward. The world dropped away as the nose of the ship turned toward the heavens above. In less than a minute, the panorama of constellations spread before them like a never-ending banquet.

Nafisa had watched enough ships come and go from her planet to understand the swiftness of this craft. Yet, she had never imagined the sensation of soaring into the skies, of seeing the millions of points of light slowly come into focus, like jewels she could reach out and touch.

"Beautiful, isn't it?"

She did not feel trapped by the vastness. Instead, she felt part of something greater. As though she could spread her arms and glide between the stars, touching their beauty, weeping at their majesty and splendor.

Nafisa turned to the pilot with new appreciation. "It's incredible."

The yellow-haired woman grinned. "You either love flying or you hate it."

"And you … you have always loved this? Flying a ship through the heavens?"

The pilot nodded enthusiastically. "Since I was a kid. My dad flew planes, but I always knew I wanted to go faster. Higher."

Something tugged at Nafisa's heart. Something like longing, if only to have had the chance to dream the kinds of dreams this woman had.

"What world are you from?"

The pilot's smile faded. "I'm not at liberty to say, ma'am."

The truth thrust home. Nafisa was a prisoner, not a guest. This woman was her jailor.

"Look. You see over there?"

Nafisa glanced where the pilot gestured. A large green and brown orb came into view from behind the moon's horizon.

"That's Duros."

The second planet. Many nights Nafisa had looked up at the glowing yellow-green star. Before now, the distant world had always been a mere point of light against the sky. She stared at the whorls and swaths of color on the sphere's surface, remembering the rhymes Saba had sung to her as a child:

Duros the land of forests so fair

Filling the world with the purest of air

Giving her people a rich fertile land

Upon which to grow; upon which to stand.

Duros a land once bountiful and free

'Til its people cut down every last living tree

Felling their future without even trying

They doomed all their children to a planet now dying.

Duros a planet deserted and lost

Man had desire, and earth paid the cost.

They took to the skies, looking back where they'd been

Hoping one day their Duros might breathe once again.

"Not very pretty," the woman added, "but readings show the atmosphere is slowly stabilizing. In another ten or twenty years, the planet might be habitable again."

Flying through the vastness of the universe, anything seemed possible.

"And that," the pilot said, pointing in the other direction, "is our destination."

They angled toward the enormous ball of blue circled in silver as if crowned sovereign over the other astral bodies.

"Welcome to Trinitos. Third planet in the solar system and home of the sky gate."

Trinitos.

Mysterious and lovely, this world would either be Nafisa's triumph or her prison. Her place of victory or her place of death.

As they neared the landing area Nafisa could see another, much larger ship. Smaller vessels hovered around the craft, zipping in and out like flies. Large crates were being unloaded and stacked, and a ramp lowered as figures emerged. Nafisa spotted the towering figure of the Ajs at once, a dark cloak swirling around him. He turned and beckoned to someone. A figure walked closer, head held high. Wide eyes revealed the woman's fear.

Nafisa's heart stuttered, belly clenching.

"Saba," she whispered.

Behind Saba, a group of people came down the ramp. Light flashed off something between them. They shuffled, not bothering to hide their terror as they took in their surroundings. A small boy clung to his mother's leg, the movement of the throng jerking her forward. With horror, Nafisa saw the chains binding the group together.

Slaves.

Anger and futility warred inside her, watching as guards led them away. Her eyes found the tall form, his face turned to look up at her, lips curled in a mocking smile. He had wanted her in a ship with windows for this moment. He wanted to be sure she saw his display. He turned to look at the ramp as one last figure emerged, and Nafisa's control shattered as understanding filled her.

Saba.

The slaves.

Father.

They were his threat. If Nafisa betrayed the Ajs, tried to strike him down or escape, they would all be sacrificed.

WEDDED – MUTAZAWIJ

متزوج

Drums rolled, their throaty voices a growl rumbling along the ground and through her bones. Nafisa walked slowly as dancers carrying horns twirled around her. The fluted instruments were made of a black material, each twisted into a spiral. Between the musicians, women dressed in flowing layers of silk dipped and whirled, bare feet stamping the ground in cadence with the drums, flat metal discs tied to their wrists with ribbons. They alternately slid the discs against each other to make soft hissing accents or clapped them together soundly to create crashing explosions.

Nafisa wondered if any of them understood the weight of what was about to happen. Were any of them Asfari? She tried to discern their faces. But the veils fell from circlets banded at the forehead rather than the nose, concealing all but their movements.

The dancers and musicians guided her along the winding stone path through the gardens outside what she could only assume was the palace of the Ajs. The great stone structure loomed, rock walls as black as the sakhra she held in her hands beneath a drape of silk. The shadow of the imposing structure touched the path. She tried to avoid it, but could not, forced along by the moving bodies of her procession. As she stepped into the shadow's murk, cold fingers scuttled up her spine. Gratefully, she emerged back into the light as they rounded a corner.

Before her, people filled the garden space. They parted like water as the dancers, drummers and horn players capered between them, carving a path. At their center, Nafisa tried to maintain her calm. This did not matter. She was still Nafisa El Farouz, defender of the sun, princess of her people. Let the Ajs parade her like a prize if such a display suited him. She must not show fear. She must not show … anything.

A pedestal stood at the front of the crowd with two chairs centered atop, one black and imposing, one small and white, both plain and unadorned. An'hlj stood beside them, garbed in traditional robes, his head dress held in place, not with a black circlet but a gold one. As if he were their sovereign.

And hers.

As the procession reached the pedestal, the dancers dispersed to the left and right. The musicians followed, continuing to play until the Ajs held up his hand. Immediately, all became quiet.

He motioned for her to come to him.

Revulsion nearly made her pull away. She forced her feet to move closer and her hand to reach out and take the one he offered. She quelled the shiver that tried to work through her at the touch of his hot skin.

He tugged her forward, up onto the platform, positioning her before the white chair, facing away from the people gathered below.

"Do not move." He turned and sat in the black chair.

Nafisa was left to stand, staring at the trees and grass, hearing the rustle of fabric as those behind her shifted like reeds in the wind. Did he think not being able to look at the guests would cause her discomfort? If so, he was mistaken. She was grateful not to see. This way, she could imagine they were as revolted as she.

Footsteps came from her left. She shifted her gaze toward the bare feet of a man in brown robes who stopped beside her.

"Bow your head." His deep voice scratched with age.

Nafisa's brows pricked in confusion, but she did as asked.

Without warning, the brown-robed man grasped a braid of her hair, jerking her head to the side. He sawed at the strands with a blade. She cried out, nearly dropping the sakhra she clutched. A second man held her firmly as the robed stranger yanked the severed braid from her hair. His grip relaxed as the braid, still threaded with pearls, dropped into a large chalice. Her head felt oddly light, leaving her off balance. Strands of hair drifted around her. One loose pearl rolled at her feet.

A rough hand grasped her arm, turning her to face An'hlj. She kept her gaze on her feet, refusing to look up at him. Silence followed, interrupted by the distinct sound of the blade reaping a second harvest. The chalice was thrust between Nafisa and the Ajs. A dark brown lock of his hair rested atop her braid.

She jerked as a flame flared to life from within the cup, burning hot and bright.

"An offering that this union might be blessed," the man in brown rasped.

Nafisa ground her teeth. This union would be anything but blessed.

Strands of hair curled and smoked as the flames devoured them. Precious pearls, like the hope of her people, singed black and crumbled to dust. The flames turned from red to white in swift intensity. The light danced, bright amid the dark mass of hair.

Was there hope to be found, even now?

A woman approached, handing a pitcher to the man in brown.

He lifted the cup high. "From the ashes, comingled, renewal."

He lowered the cup, and poured the liquid from the pitcher into the ashes. Wine, red as blood, filled the chalice, mixing with the soot. Charred material floated, swirling across the surface. Nafisa stared in horror as the man offered the cup to An'hlj. His burning eyes stared into hers as he swallowed the filthy concoction.

Her stomach turned as she awaited the certainty of what would come next. She looked into the hard face of the man holding the chalice. His black eyes did not glow as his master's did, but their stony indifference was just as terrible.

"Drink." The Ajs leaned close, his breath hot and fetid.

What would happen when An'hlj's ashes washed down her throat mingled with her own? The tendrils of his magic inside her writhed, as if confirming to drink would be her undoing.

Nafisa trembled. Eloah, show your hand. Pardon me from this.

Eloah was silent. Could this truly be his will?

"Drink." Threats suffused his command.

If she refused, the lives of everyone she loved would be held forfeit. If she accepted, her own life was as good as ended.

The brown-robed man thrust the cup against her hand. She let her fingers curl around the metal. No matter if fouled wine dripped onto her silks. The stain would be an appropriate decoration for this defilement of a wedding.

She could not think of what was happening or what would come next. She must protect her people in the only way she could.

She lifted the cup to her lips, careful not to inhale the burnt, putrid scent. She tilted the chalice, eyes following the ruby trail of liquid as it slid toward her lips.

Only wine, nothing more. A fine, red wine to mark the occasion.

Nafisa steeled herself and drank.

SHADOWS – ALZILAL

الظلال

The shadows came from everywhere. They seeped from between the trees and slithered across the grass. Like eyeless vipers they advanced directly toward her, as if able to sense the rising heat within. The wine trickled down the back of her throat, leaving a scorching trail. When An'hlj touched her a moment later, his hand hot against her arm, she understood the blaze came from him—from the part of him she had ingested. The Ajs was a fire. He burned and consumed, leaving nothing in his wake but destruction and cinders.

He turned her to face forward. The ground tilted. His face blurred, yellow eyes burning like lamps, strange star-shaped irises backlit by the glow.

"Sit."

Here was a command she could agree with. Her legs buckled, dropping her into the seat with a thud. She feared he would rage at her, but he smiled instead. A triumphant, eager smile that made her want to slap the sneer from his face. He sat beside her, looking out at the people. Nafisa turned to look as well, frowning as the shapes expanded and contracted, expanded and contracted.

Like the sakhra.

Like the heart.

Nafisa gasped. She'd nearly forgotten she still clutched the black rock. As if sensing her attention, the stone pulsed against her skin, moving in rhythm with her vision. Moving in rhythm with her heartbeat.

Her heart throbbed in sync with his.

Disgust washed through her. She blinked, trying to push back the effect and saw the man still holding the chalice step onto the platform.

She would not drink again. She refused.

But, the man didn't extend the cup. Instead, he dipped in a cloth, coloring the material a blackened, deep red. He tied one end of the sullied linen around the right wrist of the Ajs. The dominant arm. He turned to her, holding the other end and reaching for her left hand. The subordinate.

No. She would not submit.

I am Nafisa El Farouz, daughter of the Shultan. My will is my own.

Movement in the crowd drew her attention. Saba! Her handmaid stared, eyes wide. She had admonished Nafisa for her words, but she'd spoken the truth. This man was a shaytan. This ceremony an abomination. A profane abasement. They had forced it down her throat and made her drink.

Now they sought to bind her to such evil. How could she allow herself to be tied to this man? To submit to his will? The act would be the last strand of a weaving which, once done, could not be undone. She wanted to rip the cloth away. To throw the cup against the ground and stamp the metal flat.

Beside Saba, someone else moved.

Father.

He was here.

His eyes flicked to the linen still proffered by the stony man who had shorn her hair and fed her ashes to drink before moving to her left hand.

He dipped his head a fraction.

Betrayal and misery flooded through her. Her shoulders slumped, caving in along with the last of her resistance. Her father wanted her to finish the ceremony. Even now, seeing what the Ajs had done, her father wanted her to marry this evil man.

The shadows reached her feet and climbed her legs. Their smoky forms rasped like rope against her skin. With a sigh of defeat she held out her arm. The man quickly tied the fabric around her wrist.

Like a shackle.

The writing shapes reached her chest and turned to slither out along her arm, lingering on the place where her flesh met the wine-stained cloth. They clustered at the linen, turning and twisting. Nafisa watched in amazement as they touched the moist cloth and burst into flame, disintegrating in a puff of ash and drifting away on the breeze.

"You are bound to your husband," the brown-robed man intoned. He turned to the Ajs. "You are bound to your wife. All that belonged to one belongs to both. All that was separate is united."

There was a smattering of applause.

The Ajs stood, lifting her from her seat as if she weighed nothing. He drew her close. "There is but one more thing we need do," he whispered, his eyes lit with depraved appetite. "Come."

His hand burned her arm with molten intensity. She expected her flesh to melt beneath his fingers. He led her off the pedestal and into the grass, heedless of the guests.

The shadow of the stone building fell over them. The snakelike phantoms still wrapped around her body whipped into a frenzy. An'hlj opened a door, pushing her ahead of him into a stone corridor lit with torches.

Into her nightmare.

The door closed behind them, shutting them in. Firelight danced and cavorted, turning shadows into monsters stretched from floor to ceiling. The smoky wraiths dove and twisted, searching for something to devour.

"Go." He pushed her along the hallway toward a small point of brightness.

Whatever was to happen would take place there. She stumbled toward the light, leaving a trail of wet footprints as sharp rocks pierced her bare feet. Shadow creatures appeared from every crack and corner, sliding down the walls and along the floor, writhing at the spots of blood she left behind. They were his evil, she knew. Living sharun. Physical manifestations of the darkness inside the Ajs. They pressed in until she could see little else.

And then the floor gave way.

She let out a startled scream as she fell, even though she should not have been surprised. This had all happened once before. Just as in her dream, the sensation of falling into space changed to one of sliding. Her back slammed against solid rock.

Only she was not on the ceiling. She lay on a slab. An'hlj leaned over her, eyes glowing, his strange four-pointed irises swollen and eager.

"What belonged to one belongs to both," he growled. "But what is separate is not combined. Not completely." He leaned close, his hot, dry tongue sliding out to flick against her face. "Not yet." His feted and sulphurous breath wafted over her. "There is one last deed."

She could not move. Could not even turn her face to look away.

His mouth widened, revealing teeth descending too far back into his throat. Rows and rows of them like rings of thorns. His jaw worked and the rings moved, teeth clicking and grinding together as he lowered his mouth toward hers.

"A kiss to seal our union," he snarled. "And your fate."

Saba had been right after all.

Fate had caught her.

DESTINY – MASIR

مصير

His lips were surprisingly, unpleasantly soft. They pressed against hers with the fleshy quality of rotted fish. Fear tremored through her at the thought of all those rows of teeth, but he did not tear into her. Instead, as his lips parted, a great pull sucked her breath away. The sensation quickly turned from bizarre to brutal as the air vacated her lungs.

Clarity shook her. An'hlj was Yunfah—one who could control the air. Not by causing gales or walking on clouds, but by stealing the breath of another.

Her body bucked and writhed, but she could not dislodge him. His eyes, mere inches from her own, were all she could see. Twin stars blurred, circling left then right. She wanted to stare at them. To watch those dancing images and let go of her fear.

Stop fighting.

No! She pressed her eyes closed, trying to pull away as his mouth covered hers like a clamp. She could not get loose. She could not breathe. Darkness pressed in against the edges of her mind.

Still the suction continued, absorbing not only her air, but her energy. Sparks of light danced through her veins, drifting out through her tissue and merging in a stream toward the mouth covering her own. Dizzy and drained, she realized the light was her magic. He would inhale it. Drink her power like a tonic. If even one spark reached his lips, she knew with a terrible certainty, her magic would indeed become his and they were all as good as dead.

She tried to pull the sparks back, to stop the flow, but to no avail. She had no strength to stop him. She was overcome. Saba would die. Her father would die.

Her people would die.

In her hands, the sakhra pulsed as despair squeezed her heart. The darkness crushed her from within even as An'hlj himself sought to devour her from without.

Remember who you are. Saba's words whispered.

Who was she? When all else was stripped away, what remained in her heart? The darkness yawned, wanting to consume her. She must not let it. She was Nafisa El Farouz, defender of the sun, princess of her people. She was zaman, the holder of time.

She focused on the sparks. Each tiny point of light multiplied, blurring together, intensifying—each particle a reflection of a greater light, a mere piece of something bigger. A memory filled her mind. The stone altar of Eloah, its sun-shaped face glowing in the afternoon light. Eloah, the Eternal God. The light of the universe.

I am the holder of time.

The pieces fit together like a perfect pezzel. The power inside her had never been hers at all. Her sparks were mirrors, reflecting the light of Eloah. His power shone through her, defender of the sun. She opened her heart and let the light burn bright, focusing outward, illuminating everything.

Nafisa opened her eyes. The Ajs hovered over her … but he was still, his inhalation frozen between unmoving lips. Even the snakelike shadows lining the cavern walls had paused, their ephemeral forms like drawings on the stone.

Time had stopped. No, that wasn't quite right. Time continued, but she had stepped outside, holding the moment fixed.

Looking from without, she could see there was little time left. Another few moments and her magic would reach An'hlj's terrible mouth and be drawn into his awful, alien throat. For surely he was a creature never before seen in all the six worlds of Baqa. A creature sustained by horror and fear, generating what power he could and stealing what he could not.

A tremor rippled through her. Her hold on this moment was slipping. Time could not be held still forever. She must act. This would be the only chance she had.

Her father's words came to her. Think carefully Nafisa, for the hearts of others are never entirely as they seem.

She looked down at the sakhra, now quiet in her hands and knew what she must do.

Carefully, she unlocked the part of herself holding the heart's dark magic at bay. Untethered, the vile energy burst free, gleefully careening into her central consciousness. Finding nothing to devour, the darkness poured through her body, seeking any opening, any passage.

Finding only one.

Nafisa released her hold on the moment. Her last breath strained from her lungs as An'hlj fought to claim it. She lay, helpless, as darkness ate at the edges of her vision, stealing the light. The Ajs reared backward, eyes glowing, mouth pulled open in a wide, triumphant smile.

Between his lips, her last breath was a dark cloud filling his mouth. The rings of teeth in his throat worked, pulling down every drop, devouring air and magic together like flesh and bone.

He blinked, his smile faltering.

His brows lowered.

There were no points of light in the breath he sucked down, only a murky, vacuous mass. Only what she had given him.

His chest heaved.

In sync, Nafisa's chest strained, pulling in a lungful of precious air, savoring the relief.

An'hlj coughed. Dark, noxious tendrils spewed from his lips. He stared at them, uncomprehending. He coughed again, a fit seizing him until he doubled over. He clawed at his chest. More darkness poured from him, viscous and thick as oil.

"What have you done to me?" His voice was garbled. He turned to her, star-like irises contracted and thin. "This is your magic?"

Slowly, relishing that she could once again control her body, she shook her head. His frown deepened for a moment, eyes widening as understanding filled him like air. Like a breath thick with sharun.

He fell back against the stone wall of the cavern with a final shuddering breath, exhaled a cloud as black as midnight, and was still.

The Ajs An'hlj was dead.

Around him, the shadows slithered and hissed, unsure which way to go.

Nafisa must do one more thing. Closing her eyes, she touched her magic. Now that she had seen the sparks, sensed them flowing through her, pulling them forward was easy. She opened her heart to them. Eloah's light poured from her in all directions. As the light touched the shadows, they puffed into ash and disappeared. The slick, oily substance evaporated, burned away by the brightness. Still Nafisa let the light shine forth, scrubbing away each trace, arms spread wide as healing warmth washed over her, filling the room like sunlight after a storm.

When she was done, there was nothing left in the cavern with her but the empty husk of what had been the Ajs. The darkness had been cleansed.

Whatever tainted magic An'hlj had brought to this place had been vanquished.

Nafisa stood, alone and free.

***

"Your move."

Nafisa reached for one of the pieces, then stayed her hand. If she moved the guard, the princess would be safe, but her shultan would be exposed. Instead, she moved the wizard, placing him in the path of one of her father's guard pieces.

His lips curved upward. "You're getting better at this, my daughter. Soon you will outplay even me."

Somehow she doubted that. Her father reclined on a pillow, his body still recovering from the hold the Ajs had had over him. Even frail, his eyes were bright. As was his mind.

"You knew, didn't you?"

He looked up at her. "Hmm?"

"Is that why you agreed I should marry him? Even when I did not wish it?"

His smile faded, the skin of his forehead creasing downward. "To deny him would have meant our destruction. Your magic is very powerful. The light of Eloah himself. Even the Ajs could not stand against such power." He moved a guard on the Stratagem board. "Still, to risk my only daughter"—he shook his head—"I prayed you would be safe." He smiled, but not as brightly as before. "Now you are the rightful keeper of the sky gate. You are the protector of the six worlds of Baqa and champion of your people."

"You saw what I could do, even when I did not."

He reached out to touch her hand. "Eloah's will can be difficult to comprehend. We become disappointed and discouraged when we do not get the answers we desire. Believing there may be a better plan is difficult when the answer is hidden from our eyes, but there is a grander design if only we have faith."

"Ah." Nafisa smiled. Faith was a word she could appreciate. Unlike fate, which could be decided against her will, faith was a choice. "You are very wise, my father."

His full grin returned. "Good, because I have an idea as to your next husband."

Nafisa threw a pillow at his head.

He ducked, his laughter filling the room around her like magic.

ABOUT THE AUTHOR

T. E. Bradford is a writer, singer-songwriter, cancer survivor, and proud wife and mother. Born and raised in Central New York (CNY), she will tell you her parents gave her the two best tools in her arsenal by reading to her and raising her in a Christian household. In spite of the long CNY winters, she continues to live there with the husband God created just for her, and the son who is her forever best story. In her heart, she feels her gift of writing is a little piece of magic, and that it is both her privilege and grandest adventure to find new ways to stretch a hand out to touch the wonder of this vast universe God created.

AUTHOR'S NOTES

This story, and the culture depicted, were drawn from a blend of various cultures. Some words are meant to be familiar, while others were based on words from other languages. Of course this story is set in the seven worlds of Baqa, so there are some unique twists to the culture, words and translations, but that's what speculative fiction is all about, after all. Taking you on a journey to lands—and worlds—unknown.

To help you navigate the Asfari world, a quick-reference glossary has been included.

QUICK-REFERENCE GLOSSARY

Asfari	English
afeaa	serpent
Ajs	leader / shaman
alqamar	moon
alssariq	thief
cimmeron	cinnamon
Eloah	God
ginjir	ginger
ma'an	water
masir	destiny
mukhfi	hidden
musalla	worship room
najima	star
najmay	astral
pezzel	puzzle
qua	power
sahar	magic
sakhra	rock
sama	sky

sharun	evil
shaytan	demon
shultan	sultan
yasimin	Jasmine
yunfah	wind / wind-walker
zaman	time / holder of time

OTHER BOOKS BY T. E. BRADFORD

Child of Prophecy

Dragon Between Worlds